# Have you seen my Potty?

by Mij Kelly and

Mary McQuillan

First published in 2007
by Hodder Children's Books

First published in paperback in 2008

Text copyright © Mij Kelly 2007
Illustration copyright © Mary McQuillan 2007

Hodder Children's Books
An imprint of Hachette Children's Group
Part of Hodder & Stoughton
Carmelite House
50 Victoria Embankment
London EC4Y 0DZ

A catalogue record of this book is available
from the British Library.

ISBN: 978 0 340 91153 2

Printed in China

An Hachette UK Company
www.hachette.co.uk

To Joseph, Thomas and William – MK

For Amy and Jake, with love – MMcQ

# Have you seen my Potty?

WRITTEN BY
**MIJ KELLY**

ILLUSTRATED BY
**MARY McQUILLAN**

Hodder
Children's
Books

This is the story of Suzy Sue
who had something
very important to do,
something important
that she did every day…

...until someone

snatched her potty away.

What a terrible thing. What an awful to-do.
Who would play such a trick
on poor Suzy Sue?

Only a rascal quite ruthless
and rotten would steal
someone's potty from
under their bottom!

'Look
what I found,
lying around
on the
ground.'

'It's a pot.'
'It's a what?'

Oh what a disaster for poor Suzy Sue
who had something
very **important** to do.

'Have you seen my potty?'
she asked the cow.
But the cow didn't
want to talk right now.

'Besides, Suzy Sue,'
the cow pointed out,
'I've no idea
what
you're talking
about!'

'What's a potty?'

'I've no idea.'

'Hurry up with the poo-pot, we're desperate here.'

Dairy Express

A

6 $\overline{L}$

'It's so easy to use.'

'No faffing, no fuss.'

'This poo-pot's a work of pure genius!'

Oh what a disaster for poor Suzy Sue
who had something
very **important** to do.

'Have you seen my potty?' she asked the horse,
who was busy just then, but said that of course
he'd not seen her potty.
He knew this because
he had no idea
what a potty was!

'What's a potty?'

'Don't ask me.'

'Hurry up with the poo-pot.'

'I need a wee.'

'No more stepping in poo wherever we go!'

'How we managed without it, we'll never know!'

Oh what a disaster for poor Suzy Sue
who had something
very
important
to do.

'Have you seen my potty?' she asked the sheep,
who was perched on top
of a small red seat.

The sheep wanted to help.
He tried to look keen.
But this potty word,
oh what did it mean?

'What's the matter with Suzy Sue?'

'Don't ask me.'

'I need a poo!'

'What an **amazing** invention!'

'What a **wonderful** device!'

'A little **privacy** would be **nice**.'

Oh what a disaster for poor Suzy Sue
who had something

very important to do.

'Have you
seen my
potty?'

she asked the goat,
who hummed and hawed
and cleared his throat.

'Beg pardon,' he said.
'Have I seen your wotty?
What is this thing
you call a potty?'

Oh what a disaster for poor Suzy Sue
who had something very **important** to do. . .

. . .something **important**
that she did **every day.**

If she couldn't find her potty…
she'd do it **anyway.**

'We've got the very thing for you.'

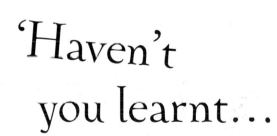

'Haven't you learnt… or have you forgotten… always poo with a poo-pot under your bottom!'

That was the story of Suzy Sue
who had something
very important to do...

'If only she'd told us she needed a poo!'